My Best Book of
Nursery Rhymes

Brown Watson

ENGLAND

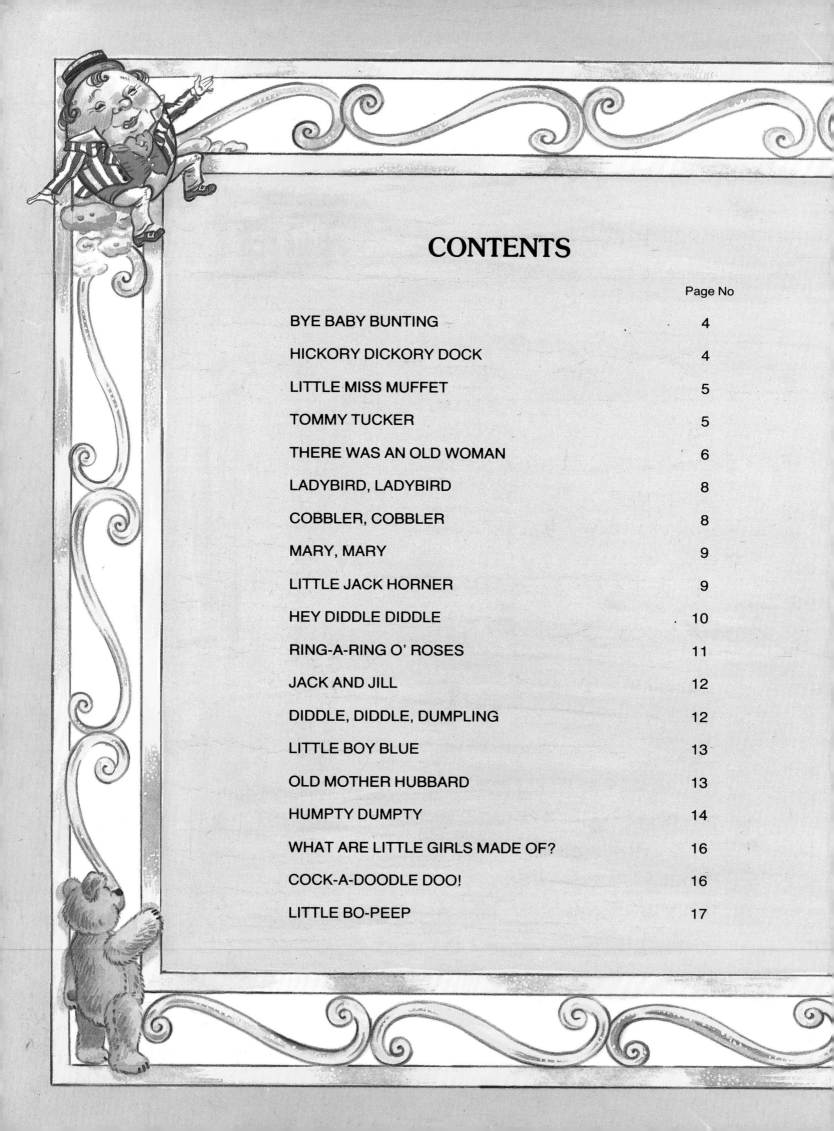

CONTENTS

BYE, BABY BUNTING

Bye, Baby Bunting,
Daddy's gone a-hunting,
Gone to get a rabbit skin
To wrap the Baby Bunting in.

HICKORY, DICKORY DOCK

Hickory, dickory dock,
The mouse ran up the clock.
The clock struck one,
The mouse ran down,
Hickory, dickory dock.

LITTLE MISS MUFFET

Little Miss Muffet
Sat on a tuffet,
Eating her curds and whey;
There came a big spider,
Who sat down beside her
And frightened Miss Muffet away.

TOMMY TUCKER

Little Tommy Tucker sang for his supper;
What shall we give him?
White bread and butter.
How shall he cut it without any knife?
How will he marry, without any wife?

5

THERE WAS AN OLD WOMAN

There was an old woman,
Who lived in a shoe,
She had so many children
She didn't know what to do;
She gave them some broth,
Without any bread,
She whipped them all soundly,
And sent them to bed.

LADYBIRD, LADYBIRD

Ladybird, ladybird,
Fly away home,
Your house is on fire
And your children all gone;
All except one,
And that's little Ann,
And she crept under
The warming pan.

COBBLER, COBBLER

Cobbler, cobbler, mend my shoe,
Get it done by half-past-two;
Stitch it up and stitch it down,
Then I'll give you half-a-crown.

MARY, MARY

Mary, Mary, quite contrary,
How does your garden grow?
With silver bells and cockle shells,
And pretty maids all in a row.

LITTLE JACK HORNER

Little Jack Horner sat in the corner,
Eating a Christmas pie;
He put in his thumb,
And pulled out a plum,
And said, "What a good boy am I!"

HEY DIDDLE DIDDLE

Hey diddle, diddle
The cat and the fiddle,
The cow jumped over the moon;
The little dog laughed
To see such sport,
And the dish ran away with the spoon.

RING-A-RING O' ROSES

Ring-a-ring o' roses,
A pocket full of posies,
A-tishoo! A-tishoo!
We all fall down.

JACK AND JILL

Jack and Jill went up the hill,
To fetch a pail of water;
Jack fell down, and broke his crown,
And Jill came tumbling after.

DIDDLE, DIDDLE, DUMPLING

Diddle, diddle, dumpling, my son John,
Went to bed with his trousers on;
One shoe off and one shoe on,
Diddle, diddle, dumpling, my son John.

12

LITTLE BOY BLUE

Little Boy Blue,
Come blow your horn;
The sheep's in the meadow,
The cow's in the corn.

Where is the boy
Who looks after the sheep?
He's under the haystack,
Fast asleep.

OLD MOTHER HUBBARD

Old Mother Hubbard
Went to the cupboard,
To get her poor doggy a bone;
But when she got there,
The cupboard was bare,
And so the poor doggy got none!

13

HUMPTY DUMPTY

Humpty Dumpty sat on a wall,
Humpty Dumpty had a great fall;
All the King's horses and all the King's men,
Couldn't put Humpty together again.

WHAT ARE LITTLE GIRLS MADE OF?

What are little girls made of, made of?
What are little girls made of?
Sugar and spice,
And all things nice,
That's what little girls are made of.

What are little boys made of, made of?
What are little boys made of?
Snips and snails,
And puppy dogs' tails,
That's what little boys
are made of.

COCK-A-DOODLE DOO!

Cock-a-doodle doo!
My dame has lost her shoe,
My master's lost his fiddling stick,
And knows not what to do.

LITTLE BO-PEEP

Little Bo-peep has lost her sheep,
And doesn't know where to find them;
Leave them alone, and they'll come home,
Bringing their tails behind them.

JACK BE NIMBLE

Jack be nimble,
Jack be quick,
Jack jump over
The candlestick.

17

RIDE A COCK-HORSE TO BANBURY CROSS

Ride a cock-horse to Banbury Cross,
To see a fine lady upon a white horse;
Rings on her fingers and bells on her toes,
She shall have music wherever she goes.

18

HERE WE GO ROUND THE MULBERRY BUSH

Here we go round the mulberry bush,
The mulberry bush, the mulberry bush,
Here we go round the mulberry bush,
On a cold and frosty morning.

GOOSEY GANDER

Goosey, goosey gander,
Where do you wander?
Upstairs and downstairs,
And in my lady's chamber,
Where I met an old man,
Who wouldn't say his prayers—
I took him by the left leg,
And threw him down the stairs.

GEORGIE PORGIE

Georgie Porgie, pudding and pie,
Kissed the girls and made them cry;
When the boys came out to play,
Georgie Porgie ran away.

ROCK-A-BYE BABY

Rock-a-bye baby,
On a tree-top,
When the wind blows
The cradle will rock.

When the bough breaks,
The cradle will fall –
Down will come baby,
Cradle and all!

TOM THE PIPER'S SON

Tom, Tom, the piper's son,
Stole a pig and away did run;
The pig was eat,
And Tom was beat,
And Tom went howling down the street.

BOYS AND GIRLS COME OUT TO PLAY!

Boys and girls come out to play,
The moon does shine as bright as day.
Leave your supper and leave your sleep,
And join your friends out in the street.
Come with a whoop and come with a call,
Come with good will or not at all.
Up the ladder and down the wall,
A half-penny loaf will serve us all;
You find milk and I'll find flour,
And we'll have a pudding in half-an-hour.

CURLY LOCKS

Curly Locks, Curly Locks, will you be mine?
You shall not wash dishes, nor yet feed the swine;
You'll sit on a cushion and sew a fine seam,
And feed upon strawberries, sugar and cream.

PUSSY CAT, PUSSY CAT

Pussy cat, pussy cat,
Where have you been?
I've been up to London,
To visit the Queen.

Pussy cat, pussy cat,
What did you there?
I frightened a little mouse,
'Neath the Queen's chair.

THE CROOKED MAN

There was a crooked man,
And he walked a crooked mile.
He found a crooked sixpence
Beside a crooked stile;

He bought a crooked cat,
Which caught a crooked mouse,
And they all lived together
In a little crooked house.

TO BED, TO BED

"To bed, to bed!" said Sleepy Head.
"Tarry a while," said Slow.
"Put on the pan," said greedy Ann.
"We'll sup before we go."

WEE WILLIE WINKIE

Wee Willie Winkie
Runs through the town,
Upstairs and downstairs
In his nightgown;
Rapping at the window,
Crying through the lock,
Are the children all in bed,
For now it's eight o'clock.

POLLY FLINDERS

Little Polly Flinders
Sat among the cinders,
Warming her pretty little toes;
Her mother came and caught her,
And smacked her little daughter,
For spoiling her nice new clothes.

MARY HAD A LITTLE LAMB

Mary had a little lamb,
Its fleece was white as snow,
And everywhere that Mary went
That lamb was sure to go.

It followed her to school one day–
That was against the rule;
It made the children laugh and play,
To see a lamb at school.

SEE-SAW MARGERY DAW

See-saw Margery Daw,
Jack shall have a new master;
Jack shall work for a penny a day,
Because he can't work any faster.

SING A SONG OF SIXPENCE

Sing a song of sixpence,
A pocket full of rye;
Four and twenty blackbirds
Baked in a pie.

When the pie was opened,
The birds began to sing;
Wasn't that a dainty dish
To set before the King.

The King was in his counting-house,
Counting out his money;
The Queen was in the parlour,
Eating bread and honey.

The maid was in the garden,
Hanging out the clothes,
When down came a blackbird
And pecked off her nose.

They sent for the King's doctor,
Who sewed it on again,
And he sewed it on so neatly,
The seam was never seen.

JACK SPRAT COULD EAT NO FAT

Jack Sprat could eat no fat,
His wife could eat no lean,
So it came to pass, between them both,
They licked the platter clean.

Jack ate all the lean,
Joan ate all the fat,
The bone they picked it clean,
Then gave it to the cat.

THERE WAS A LITTLE GIRL

There was a little girl and she had a little curl,
Right in the middle of her forehead;
When she was good, she was very, very good,
But when she was bad, she was horrid!

SIMPLE SIMON

Simple Simon met a pieman,
Going to the fair;
Said Simple Simon to the pieman:
"Let me taste your ware."
Said the pieman to Simple Simon:
"Show me first your penny."
Said Simple Simon to the pieman:
"Indeed, I have not any."

POLLY PUT THE KETTLE ON

Polly put the kettle on,
Polly put the kettle on,
Polly put the kettle on,
We'll all have tea.

Sukey take it off again,
Sukey take it off again,
Sukey take it off again,
They've all gone home.

THREE BLIND MICE

Three blind mice, three blind mice,
See how they run, see how they run!
They all ran after the farmer's wife,
Who cut off their tails with the carving knife,
Did you ever see such a thing in your life,
As three blind mice?